FAERIEGROUND

The Shadows

Book Two

BY BETH BRACKEN AND KAY FRASER

ILLUSTRATED BY ODESSA SAWYER

STONE ARCH BOOKS

a capstone imprint

FAERIEGROUND IS PUBLISHED BY
STONE ARCH BOOKS
A CAPSTONE IMPRINT
1710 ROE CREST DRIVE
NORTH MANKATO, MINNESOTA 56003
WWW.CAPSTONEPUB.COM

LIBRARY OF CONGRESS CATALOGING-IN-
PUBLICATION DATA IS AVAILABLE ON THE
LIBRARY OF CONGRESS WEBSITE.

LIBRARY BINDING: 978-1-4342-3306-6

SUMMARY: SOLI MUST TRY TO FIND LUCY,
WHO IS TRAPPED IN FAERIEGROUND

BOOK DESIGN BY K. FRASER
ALL PHOTOS © SHUTTERSTOCK WITH THESE
EXCEPTIONS: AUTHOR PORTRAIT © K FRASER
AND ILLUSTRATOR PORTRAIT © ODESSA
SAWYER

PRINTED IN THE UNITED STATES OF AMERICA
IN STEVENS POINT, WISCONSIN.
052013
007383R

For Valarie, who wished me away, and wished me home. -b
For the Fraser sisters: you are all a mother could wish for. -k

Long ago, a kingdom was
founded in Willow Forest . . . .

Over time, the human village and the faerie kingdom grew further apart. Some humans began to spread rumors that the faeries were evil. Some faeries believed that the humans were murderers. The balance shifted. Things were changing.

And then there was a new queen of the faeries.

Calandra.

Chapter 1

Soli

There's a rock in my hand when I wake up.

Yesterday comes rushing back. The wish. The light. Lucy disappearing. Did it happen?

I stare at the rock. Yes. It happened. Lucy kissed Jaleel, and because of that, I made a wish that she'd disappear, and because of that, she did.

I get ready for school. I try to forget that Lucy disappeared. I try to forget it's my fault. I try to forget about the wish I made in the woods. Still, I put the rock in my pocket.

What do I do now? Who would believe me?

I can't go to school. I can't keep quiet, or pretend to be normal. I can't pretend I didn't wish my friend away. So instead of going to school, I go to Lucy's house.

The rock is a weight in my pocket while I run there, traveling a path I've traveled a thousand times. Ten thousand, maybe. More.

I don't take the shortcut through the woods. I never liked to take it alone. And right now, I'm afraid of the woods. I don't ever want to go back there. I never dreamed the stories could be true.

At Lucy's house, I stand on the step. What can I tell Andria? What will she already know? Will she be worried? Will she blame me?

I would. I do, I do blame myself.

Before I can even knock, the front door opens wide. I hold my breath.

Lucy's mom looks at me the way a mother would look at a daughter. She's not my mother, but she might as well be. "Hello, Soli," she says. "I've been waiting for you."

Chapter 2

Lucy

I'm a prisoner.

The fairies want me for something, but I don't know what. It's too dark to see anything where I am, here, in the shadows. My prison is dark and smells like death. I touch the walls in the dark and feel only wet stone. Gross. There's no way out.

Then my hand falls on a body. "Watch it," a voice says. The body moves away.

"Who's there?" I whisper.

"Keep quiet," the boy says. "Don't remind them you're here."

I move back to my corner. "Who are you?" I ask. I try to keep my voice from shaking, but it isn't easy. I'm afraid, and my voice betrays me.

From the other side of the cell, the voice whispers, "My name is Kheelan. Don't be scared. I'm a prisoner too."

"I'm Lucy," I say.

"I know who you are," he says. "The light girl."

What? Light?

My hair, maybe. But how does he know who I

am? Who's told him about me?

"What do they want from me?" I ask.

"Queen Calandra wants the dark one.

Your friend," Kheelan says. "The one in the

shadows."

I forget to whisper. Instead, I laugh. "Soli?" I

ask. "Dark?"

Soli isn't dark. Soli isn't dark at all.

Chapter 3

Lucy

When we were five, we promised to be best friends forever.

We pretended we were having a fairy

ceremony, even though Soli didn't believe in

them. Because I wouldn't let her.

Instead, I made it a game. We carved our

names in the shadows of an old willow tree.

The tree still stands in Willow Forest.

Once, when we were small, Soli found a

wounded bird by our tree house. She took

it in. She fed the bird and kept it warm. She

made a little bed for it in a box. She named it

Henrietta.

Soli sang to the bird, some sweet old lullaby

her mother must have sung to her.

Everything will heal.

Everyone will feel

Better, in the morning.

Better, in the morning.

Soon, the bird flew away. Soli gave that bird its life back.

She gave me my life back too, when my dad died. I couldn't talk about it. Not to my mom, not to Soli, not to anyone.

After the funeral, Soli came to my house. "You don't have to talk," she told me. "But we need to be together. And soon you'll feel better. I promise."

We stayed in my room, and she hummed, and she stroked my hair.

Better, in the morning.

She was right. We need to be together. Best friends forever. And look at us now. Fighting over a boy, a boy I barely even cared about.

Chapter 4

Lucy

"Why are you here?" I ask the boy in the other corner of the cell.

"Queen Calandra thinks I'm rebellious," Kheelan says. I can hear the smile in his voice. "So she's punishing me."

"I guess that makes two of us," I mutter.

"Will your friend come for you?" Kheelan asks.

"She's my best friend," I say. I think of our names on the old tree. "She'll never leave me here."

"That's part of her plan," he says. "The queen's."

"Who is she, anyway?" I ask.

"Calandra?" Kheelan says. "Ah, she's just
the queen. She is many long stories, not all
of them true. Most of them with unhappy
endings."

"Is she dangerous?" I ask.

Kheelan laughs. "Of course," he says. "But like
anything else, she only has power if you let her
have it."

"I'm afraid," I whisper.

I feel Kheelan's fingers grasping mine. "Don't be," he says.

A heavy door opens. We move apart. Light creeps in, blinding me. "The queen will see you now," a deep voice says. Hands grab my shoulders. "Get up," the man says.

I stand up and Kheelan quickly grabs my hand. "Don't let her break you," he whispers. "Be strong, Lucy." He squeezes my fingers, and then lets go.

The guard drags me out from the dark.

Chapter 5

Soli

Lucy's mother looks terrible.

"Hi, Andria," I say.

"Do you know where she is?" Lucy's mom asks. She's worried. Of course she is. I forget sometimes that I'm not Lucy's whole world.

I look around. "Can I come in?" I ask.

"Of course," Andria says. "I'm sorry. Yes. Please come in."

I sit down on the couch. Lucy and I have sat here so many times. Will we ever sit together again?

"So?" Andria asks. "Where is she? I'm so worried about her."

"I don't know," I say.

Andria's face turns pale. "When is the last time you saw her?" she asks.

Can I tell her the truth? That in the forest, I wished her daughter away, and it worked? That I think faeries took her? That they sent me a message? Lucy always pretended not to believe in faeries, but I know Lucy's mom does.

"Lucy is gone because I wished her away," I blurt out.

"What?" Andria whispers. Her eyes grow wide.

"We were in the forest," I say. "Yesterday, after school. I was mad, and . . . " Tears sting my eyes. "I'm sorry," I whisper.

Lucy's mom closes the window. Then she pulls the blinds. Then she locks the door. "Listen to me very carefully," she says. "Did they try contacting you?"

I pull the rock out of my pocket. Andria's face is white. "This came through my window," I tell her. "Lucy's name is on it." I hold it out to her.

Andria grabs the rock. She turns it over in her hands. She rubs her thumb across Lucy's name. "Do you know what it says?" I ask.

Andria reads the strange letters. "A faerie's contract has been made. Come to Willow's Gate to find Lucy." She swallows hard. "It's the faerie language," she tells me.

"I can't believe they're real," I say.

"Oh, they're very real," Andria says. Something in her voice tells me to not question her.

"How do we get her back?" I ask.

Andria sighs. "We don't, Soli. " she says. "You do. You're the only way."

"How?" I whisper.

"You have to go to them," she tells me. "No one else can do this."

"What do I do?" I ask, pretending to be brave.

"Go to the depths of Willow Forest alone," she tells me. "Find a four-leafed clover. Then pull each of its leaves. When they're gone, say your wish."

"No way," I say. "I'm never wishing in the forest again."

"You need to wish to see a faerie. Otherwise the door will be invisible to you," Andria explains. "And if the door stays invisible, we'll never get Lucy back."

"Okay," I whisper. Whatever it takes. A hunt
for a four-leafed clover in the middle of the
woods.

Andria gazes at me. Then she takes off her
necklace. A silver shape hangs from a thin
silver strand.

"Take this," she says. "It will protect you."

"It's beautiful," I say, gazing at the delicate
necklace. "Where did you get it? How do you
know it will keep me safe?"

Andria's face turns dark. "An old friend gave it to me for doing her a favor," she says. "Don't tell any of the faeries about it. It might be worth something to them. You might be able to trade it. I'm not sure what it means to them. My friend never told me. But save it for a last resort and don't give it to the queen." She stands up. "Now. Go."

I look down at the charm on the chain. It's a four-leafed clover trapped inside a three-ring circle. Then I secure the chain around my neck. The charm drops down to my heart, and I tuck it inside my shirt.

"What should I do once I'm there?" I ask. "In the faerieground, I mean."

"Find the queen's secret," she says. "The wish that keeps her captive there. But be careful. She's crafty. She'll trick you."

I stand to leave, but Andria stops me. "I almost forgot. There's something else you might need," she says.

She rummages in a closet and pulls out a jar. Just a simple old glass jar.

"What is this for?" I ask.

Andria shrugs. "It's always good to have a jar. You'll see."

I put the jar in my knapsack.

"Bring her back," Andria whispers.

The next thing I know, I'm running toward Willow Forest.

Chapter 6

Soli

Once we were in the woods, Lucy and I, playing a game.

I don't remember what the game was, only
that I was hiding, and Lucy was supposed to
find me.

It grew dark. Cold. I kept waiting.

The woods, once a playground, became scary.
I waited and waited and waited.

I knew my way out of the woods. I knew
the woods like I knew my own face, or my
mother's face. I knew exactly where I was and
how to get home from there.

So as the woods became darker and darker
and colder and colder, I could have stood up,
brushed the dirt off my clothes, and walked
home. I would not have been afraid.

That's not what I did.

I believed Lucy would find me.

And she did.

Chapter 7

Lucy

When you think of faeries,
you think of light.

Light. Sweetness. Joy.

Queen Calandra's palace has none of

those things. It's cold and damp and dark.

Spiderwebs cling to the walls.

The guard brings me to a stone-walled room.

Candles burn on a table. There is a throne.

"She is here," the guard says. He pushes me

forward. Then the doors slam behind me.

"Do you have it?" a woman's voice asks, rising

from the near shadows.

"Have what?" I ask. I look down at myself. I have nothing except my clothes.

"The necklace. Your mother's necklace," the queen says.

Then I see her. Queen Calandra. She is beautiful and dangerous. She doesn't look like the other faeries. She is more solid, and also more terrifying.

"The necklace!" the queen snaps. Her voice is a whip bent across the room.

"No, I don't have it," I say. "She never takes it off."

It's the truth. My mother has worn that necklace forever. As long as I can remember, anyway.

"Then you'll have to wait until someone brings it," the queen says. "You may as well make yourself at home in the prison."

"This isn't my home," I say. "Please, just let me go. I can make sure you get what you want."

"No," the queen says. "I don't trust humans."

Then her eyes glow. "Unless you make a wish,

that is."

"What kind of wish?" I ask.

"Wish for that friend of yours to take your

place," she says. "Trade places with your friend.

Send her here, free yourself."

"I could never do that to Soli," I whisper. "If

that is my only way out, there is no way out." I

won't betray Soli, not again, not ever.

"Imagine being back home, the comfort," the queen says. Her voice drips with sweetness.

"Stop it," I say. "Stop."

"Your own bed. How soft it would be, after a night spent on stone! How warm, how welcome! Wouldn't you love to sleep in your own room again, your mother in the next room, protecting you?" the queen whispers, a sugar-spun smile crossing her face like a flicker.

"Stop," I moan.

"The gentle arms of your mother, embracing you," she says. "Your mother! All you have to do is wish her here, your friend. Soledad. And then you can be with your mother again. A simple trade. An easy bargain."

"I won't do it," I say. I make my voice as strong as I can. Strong like my mother. "I won't do that to Soli."

"She wished you away!" the queen says. The honey is gone from her voice.

"I'm not her," I say.

The queen laughs. "No," she says. "No, you're

not. But you're close."

Chapter 8

Soli

In Willow Forest, I stop running.

I find the place where Lucy and I were
yesterday. The undergrowth is matted where
we sat, where we fought.

I know wishes are heard here.

I reach up and touch the charm around my
neck. Find a four-leafed clover? This could take
hours.

I drop to my knees. It's dark in the forest, even
though it's still morning. As I pick through
the clover, one firefly blinks nearby. Soon, it's
joined by another, then another.

They cluster over a patch of clover in the

shadows beneath a thick, old tree.

I set down my backpack and hear the clunk of

Andria's jar, hitting the ground.

When we were little, Lucy and I loved

trapping fireflies in jars. Some kids squashed

the bugs and used their guts to paint lit words.

The light only lasted a minute.

Lucy and I didn't want to hurt the fireflies. We

just thought they were beautiful.

When we put them in jars, they'd blink at us,

like an old-time message. Lucy and I would

make up meanings, pretend we knew what the

fireflies were saying.

Now, without Lucy, I gaze at the fireflies.

There are more now, maybe a dozen. Their

lights flash in rhythm over a patch of clover.

I reach out my hand, but none fly to me. They

stay where they are.

When I walk over, they swarm away. I reach

down, and the first thing my fingers touch is a

four-leafed clover.

A tangle of fireflies is caught in my hair.

And when I open my backpack, Andria's jar is full of fireflies, and the lid is tightly sealed.

I close my eyes, pulling the clover leaves one by one. "I wish to see faeries," I whisper. I pour my heart into the wish. I wish it more than I've ever wished anything.

I hear a whisper.

"Follow."

Chapter 9

Lucy

The guard throws me back
into the cold stone room
where Kheelan still waits.

In the light from the opened door, I can see him, bound by iron chains to the wall.

After the door slams shut, we are blind again. But only for a moment. There's a tiny window high above Kheelan's head. I wouldn't even think of escaping—it's only a few inches tall and a few inches wide. But now that the sun is out, enough light streams in to see by.

He has dark hair and eyes. In a way, he reminds me of Soli. The way her gaze feels hot, almost. Like she can see inside me. Kheelan's gaze feels like that, too.

"You're back," he says. "How was it?"

"I don't know," I say. "I think I made her mad."

He nods. "But you didn't do what she asked," he says.

"No," I say. "No, I didn't."

"That's good," Kheelan says. "With Queen Calandra, it's never just what she says. Never just the one promise. It ends up being a million horrible things, but you already agreed, and you can't take it back."

"You can't take back a wish?" I ask.

"No," Kheelan says. "Never. It's a bond between faeries, a contract."

"Between faeries?" I repeat. "But Soli and I aren't faeries."

Kheelan smiles. His smile looks like Soli's, too.

Chapter 10

Soli

The fireflies guide me.

The woods grow darker. Soon, I stand in front of an old willow tree. Lucy and I carved our names into that tree's trunk, close to the ground, in the shadows.

I bend and see that our names are still there. My finger traces the letters of our names.

"What do you want?" a voice asks. I jump up and look around, but no one is there.

"What do you want?" the voice repeats. The tree's branches sprawl in all directions, gating me in.

"Um, I got a message. See?" I say, taking the rock from my pocket.

"They're waiting for you," the voice tells me. The tree creaks at its roots. A door opens. "You may enter, Soli Meddow," the voice whispers.

I'm scared to go in. It's dark and scary in there. Unknown.

Well, not totally unknown. I know two things.

First, that Lucy is in there.

And second, that we are supposed to be

together.

I take a deep breath, close my eyes, and step

into the darkness.

Chapter 11

Lucy

I cry myself to sleep on the stone floor of Queen Calandra's prison.

I dream I'm back at school, yelling at Jaleel. He looks scared and shocked. I scream at him, over and over. He tries to run away, but he can't. I try to run away, but I can't. I am made to stand there, yelling, tears falling down my face and collecting in a puddle at my feet.

I dream I'm at home, in my room, in my bed, in my blankets. I can hear my mother's voice. She's talking about me. Saying I'm missing, saying she doesn't know where I am, saying I'm gone. Then she says she doesn't care, and she laughs, and she sounds happy. Free.

I dream I am at my father's funeral.

I'm terrified and sad, and I can't find Soli.

When I ask my mother where she is, my mother says she's never heard of anyone named Soli, who would name a child Soli, what kind of name is that anyway?

When I try to remind her of Soli, my almost-sister, my best friend, my mother just laughs and laughs and laughs.

I dream I'm in the woods, running after Soli.

I know she's angry with me. I chase her and chase her through the woods, ending up at the old willow tree where our names are carved. When she turns around and sees my face, she smiles, and she stretches her hands out. I run to hug her, and just as I'm about to wrap my arms around her, she disappears.

Chapter 12

Soli

I'm here.

And I'm ready to get my friend back.

Whatever it takes.

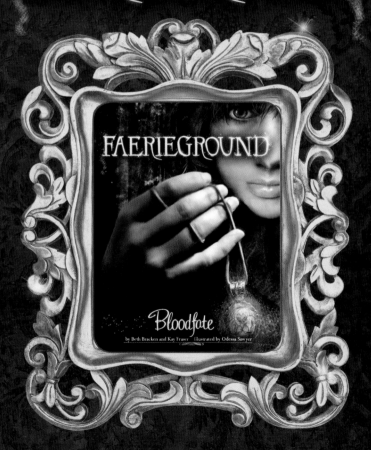

Find out what's next . . .

FAERIEGROUND

FAERIEGROUND

Bloodfate

by Beth Bracken and Kay Fraser   Illustrated by Odessa Sawyer

Fate can't be escaped.

Soledad and Lucy have never thought about their own fates. Their lives were simple, full of fun and games and school and friends. Ordinary lives lived by ordinary girls. But once they entered the faerieground, things changed.

Choices have brought Soli and Lucy here. Lucy chose to kiss the boy Soli liked, and Soli chose to wish her best friend away. But now they have no choice. Lucy must wait, imprisoned. Soli must try to find her. And as they do those things, they learn new truths about themselves—and each other.

Beth & Kay

Kay Fraser and Beth Bracken are a designer-editor team in Minnesota.

Kay is from Buenos Aires. She left home at eighteen and moved to North Dakota—basically the exact opposite of Argentina. These days, she designs books, writes, makes tea for her husband, and drives her daughters to their dance lessons.

Beth and her husband live in a tiny, crowded bungalow with their son, Sam, and their Jack Russell terrier, Harry. She spends her time editing, reading, daydreaming, and rearranging her furniture.

Kay and Beth both love dark chocolate, Buffy, and tea.

Odessa

Odessa Sawyer is an illustrator from Santa Fe, New Mexico. She works mainly in digital mixed media, utilizing digital painting, photography, and traditional pen and ink.

Odessa's work has graced the book covers of many top publishing houses, and she has also done work for various film and television projects, posters, and album covers.

Highly influenced by fantasy, fairy tales, fashion and classic horror, Odessa's work celebrates a whimsical, dreamy and vibrant quality.